THE WORLD OF PETER RABBIT™

Sticker Activity Book

Hop, Skip and Stick

THIS BOOK BELONGS TO

....

Use your **STICKERS** to decorate this page!

Based on the books by
BEATRIX POTTER

Spring Has Sprung!

It's early one morning and the rabbits are going for a walk.
Use your stickers to add Peter and his family.
Then fill the woods with birds, bugs, flowers and butterflies.

Beautiful Blooms

Flopsy, Mopsy and Cotton-tail stop to pick flowers in the sunshine.
Use your stickers to finish the jigsaw.

Bunny Trails

Benjamin wants to join the fun but which trail leads to his cousins? Stick on some friendly woodland animals for him to meet along the way.

Woodland Wings

Look at the bugs they've spotted! Each one is missing one half of their fluttering wings. Look at your stickers to find and match up each pair.

DRAGONFLY

CABBAGE WHITE BUTTERFLY

LADYBIRD

SMALL TORTOISESHELL BUTTERFLY

Peter's Pals

Look at these rows of friends. Use your stickers to complete each pattern.

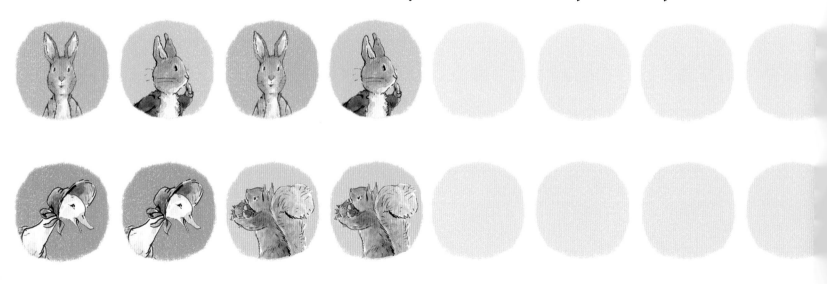

Sticky Shadows

The rabbits are hopping about in the sunshine. Use your stickers to complete this sunny scene. How many animals can you count?

Peter's Vegetable Patch

Now Peter has run to the garden. Can you give him his spade?
Don't forget to stick in lots of plants, animals and garden tools, too.

Garden Guests

Who else is in the garden today? Choose the stickers
that match these descriptions and find out who's who!

I like to waddle through the garden
in my pink shawl and blue bonnet.
WHO AM I?

I can scamper quickly through
the trees, hunting for nuts.
WHO AM I?

My little black nose goes sniffle, sniffle,
snuffle and I am covered in prickles.
WHO AM I?

I'm Peter's cousin. I like gathering
onions in Mr McGregor's garden.
WHO AM I?

We're Peter's sisters. We wear red cloaks
and we like to go blackberry picking.
WHO ARE WE?

Duckling Differences

Peter Rabbit has spotted Jemima's ducklings.
There are six differences to find. Use your stickers
to make the bottom picture match the top one.

Quack the Code

Who else could be looking for the ducklings on this beautiful spring day?
Use the yellow alphabet to find the correct green letter to crack the code.
Then add a sticker to reunite the character and the ducklings.

A	B	C	D	E	F	G	H	I	J	K	L	M	N	O	P	Q	R	S	T	U	V	W	X	Y	Z
Z	Y	X	W	V	U	T	S	R	Q	P	O	N	M	L	K	J	I	H	G	F	E	D	C	B	A

Q V N R N Z   K F W W O V - W F X P

_ _ E _ _ _ _   _ U _ _ _ E ⁻ _ U _ _

Hide and Shop

Peter and Benjamin go to buy some currant buns from Ginger and Pickles' shop.
Place a number sticker by each iced bun – there are five to find!
Then use your stickers to add more shoppers to the scene and stack the shelves.

Title Page

Spring Has Sprung!

Beautiful Blooms

Bunny Trails

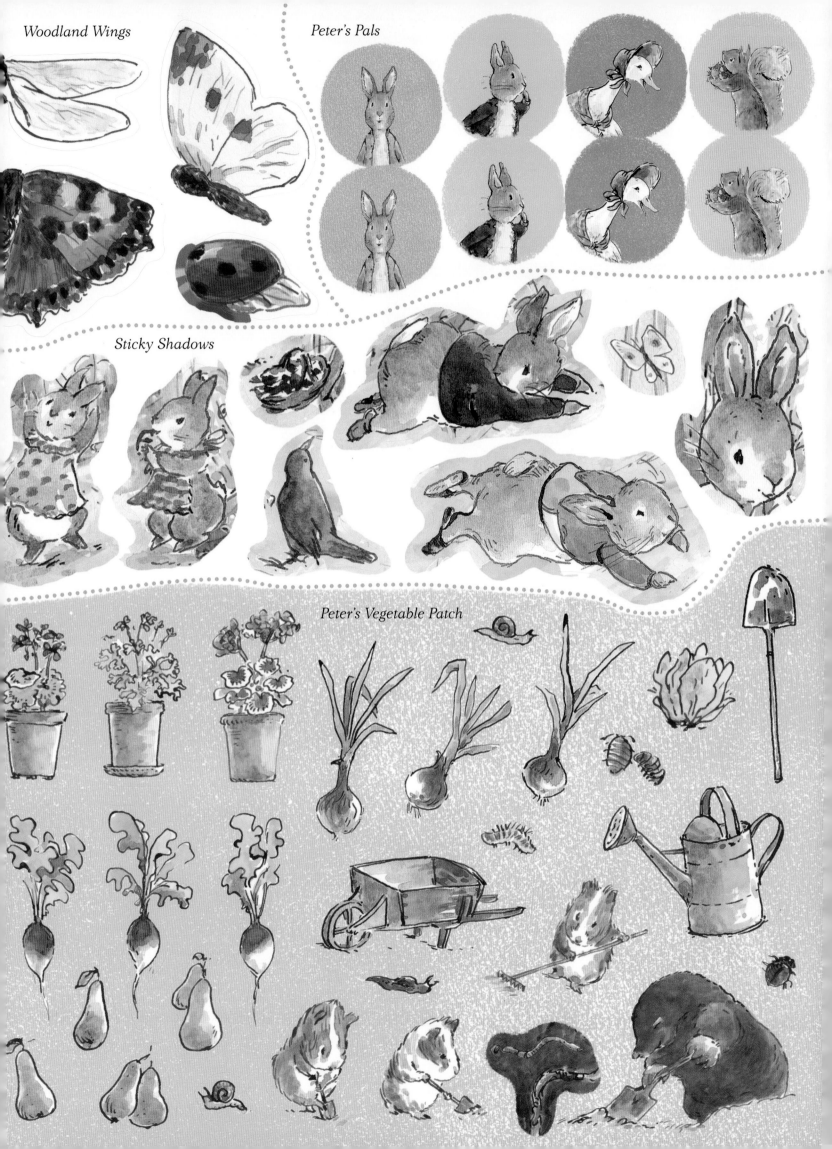

Woodland Wings

Peter's Pals

Sticky Shadows

Peter's Vegetable Patch

Garden Guests

Quack the Code

Duckling Differences

Hide and Shop

Hide and Shop

Spring Fair

Fun at the Fair

Rabbit Race

Peter

Benjamin Bunny

Mopsy

Cotton-tail

Flopsy

Party Animals

Nature Trail

Picnic Wordsearch

Party Time!

Bunny Burrow

Bedtime Bunny!

Spring Fair

On the way home from shopping, Peter and Benjamin spot a travelling funfair. Add stickers of the bunnies and the fair, then guide Peter and Benjamin through the hedgerow maze.

Fun at the Fair

They've found it! And now Peter and Benjamin have snuck under the fence to explore. Use your stickers to complete this busy funfair scene.

Rabbit Race

After the rabbits leave the fair they play chase. Which bunny will win the race?
Play this game with your friends. Then decorate the board with stickers.

Start

1

2

You trip over
a toadstool.
MISS A GO

4

Samuel Whiskers
helps you race ahead.
HAVE ANOTHER GO.

19

18

17

21

22

YOU WILL NEED:
A die
5 counters – find stickers of Peter,
Benjamin and the triplets and
fold them to make the counters.

You spot
Mr. McGregor
and hide.
MISS A GO.

24

25

A duckling stops
to say, "hello".
**GO BACK
TWO STEPS.**

Squirrel Nutkin
has dropped his nuts.
MISS A GO.

8

6

9

5

10

HOW TO PLAY:

The youngest player rolls the die first
and moves the correct number of places.
Take it in turns to roll the die and
follow the instructions on the stepping stones.
The first bunny back to the burrow is the winner!

11

Jemima Puddle-duck
shows you a shortcut.
**MOVE FORWARD
FOUR STEPS.**

16

You meet
a helpful mole.
**THROW THE
DIE AGAIN.**

14

13

27

28

29

30

Finish

Party Animals

Today is the animals' spring gathering. Use your stickers to help everyone look their party best. Don't forget to add some party stickers, too!

PETER

FLOPSY

MOPSY

COTTON-TAIL

JEMIMA PUDDLE-DUCK

BENJAMIN BUNNY

Nature Trail

The woods are full of colourful woodland animals.
Add stickers of the party pals and the creatures
they see as they head to their spring celebration.

Which yellow insect
is buzzing by the
yellow flowers?

Someone green and
wriggly is munching a
crispy green leaf in the tree.

Who is this red creature
flying over a red toadstool?
Can you count her spots?

Which blue insect
is hovering over the
shimmering blue pond?

Picnic Wordsearch

Everyone has brought some picnic food to the party. Can you find these ten items in the grid? When you find a word, add the matching sticker.

ONIONS

TEA

CAKE

PEARS

JUICE

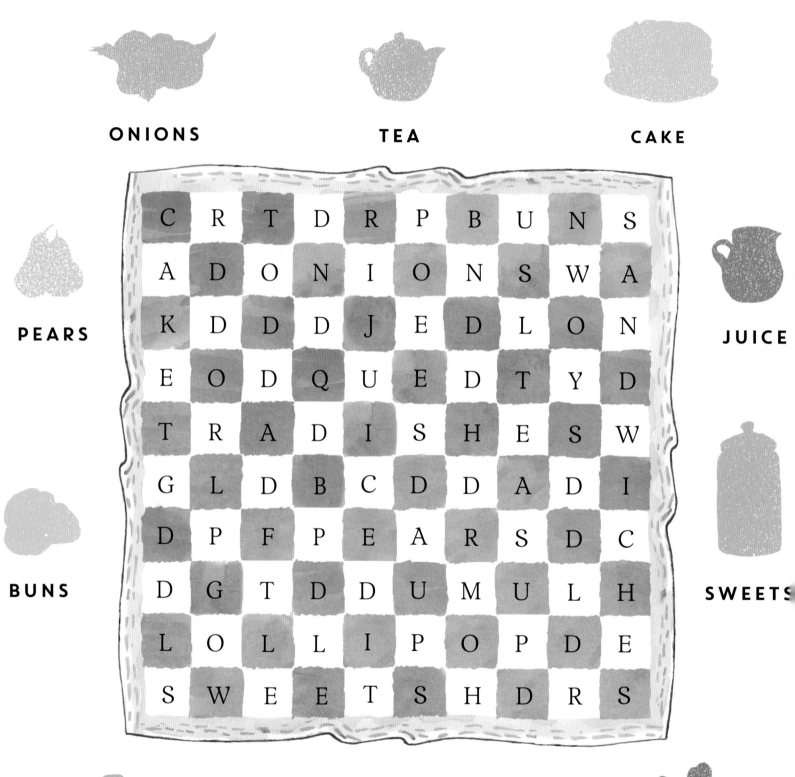

C	R	T	D	R	P	B	U	N	S
A	D	O	N	I	O	N	S	W	A
K	D	D	D	J	E	D	L	O	N
E	O	D	Q	U	E	D	T	Y	D
T	R	A	D	I	S	H	E	S	W
G	L	D	B	C	D	D	A	D	I
D	P	F	P	E	A	R	S	D	C
D	G	T	D	D	U	M	U	L	H
L	O	L	L	I	P	O	P	D	E
S	W	E	E	T	S	H	D	R	S

BUNS

SWEETS

LOLLIPOP

SANDWICHES

RADISHES

Party Time!

The animals are all having fun at the spring party.
Use your stickers to finish the jigsaw.

Bunny Burrow

After a busy day, Peter and his family are back inside their cosy burrow.
Use your stickers to complete this picture of their happy home.

Bedtime Bunny!

Now use your stickers to add Peter tucked up in bed with his favourite toy.
Add some other night-time stickers and fill the sky with stars! How many stars can you count?

Answers

Bunny Trails

Peter's Pals

Duckling Differences

Quack the Code
JEMIMA PUDDLE-DUCK
is looking for the ducklings.

Spring Fair

Picnic Wordsearch